For Constantine
—M. C.

For my big brother Gary
—B. K.

Henry Holt and Company, LLC
*Publishers since 1866*
175 Fifth Avenue
New York, New York 10010
www.HenryHoltKids.com

Library of Congress Cataloging-in-Publication Data
Cuyler, Margery.
The little dump truck / Margery Cuyler ; illustrated by Bob Kolar.
p.     cm.
"Christy Ottaviano Books."
Summary: A happy little dump truck, driven by Hard Hat Pete, hauls stones,
rocks, and debris from a construction site to a landfill.
ISBN-13: 978-0-8050-8281-4 / ISBN-10: 0-8050-8281-6
[1. Stories in rhyme.  2. Dump trucks—Fiction.  3. Trucks—Fiction.]  I. Kolar, Bob, ill.  II. Title.
PZ8.3.C99Lit 2009     [E]—dc22     2008036811

First Edition—2009 / Designed by Véronique Lefevre Sweet
Printed in China on acid-free paper. ∞
This artist used Adobe Illustrator on a Macintosh computer
to create the illustrations for this book.

1   3   5   7   9   10   8   6   4   2

# The Little DUMP Truck

Margery Cuyler

illustrated by Bob Kolar

Christy Ottaviano Books

Henry Holt and Company · New York

I'm a little dump truck
run by Hard Hat Pete,
rattle-rattle-clatter,
driving down the street.

I'm a little dump truck
hauling stones and rocks,
bumping, bouncing, thumping,
crossing city blocks.

I'm a little dump truck
turning at the light,
slowing, braking, stopping
at the building site.

I'm a little dump truck
parking in the road,
RRR-RRR-RRR,
dumping out my load.

I'm a little dump truck
watching workers build,
forklifts lifting beams,
big hole being filled.

I'm a little dump truck
waiting for debris.
Excavator scoops—
drops dirt into me!

I'm a little dump truck
carting out the trash.
On and off, on and off,
warning red lights flash.

I'm a little dump truck
driving down Route Ten,
heading for the landfill
to unload again.

I'm a little dump truck
backing to the right,
tipping down my dumper
at the garbage site.

I'm a little dump truck
leaving through the gate,
riding down the highway
to another state.

I'm a little dump truck
stopping to get gas.
Hard Hat Pete drinks coffee,
other truckers pass.

I'm a little dump truck
working hard each day.
Back and forth, back and forth,
I love my job—Hooray!